STARRING LUCILLE

by
Kathryn Lasky

illustrated by
Marylin Hafner

Alfred A. Knopf New York

For Meribah—K.L.

For Katherine, Sylvia, and Irving,
who are dancing with the stars—M.H.

THIS IS A BORZOI BOOK PUBLISHED BY ALFRED A. KNOPF

Text copyright © 2001 by Kathryn Lasky
Illustrations copyright © 2001 by Marylin Hafner

www.randomhouse.com/kids

Library of Congress Cataloging-in-Publication Data
Kathryn Lasky.
Starring Lucille / by Kathryn Lasky ; illustrated by Marylin Hafner. — 1st ed.
p. cm.
SUMMARY: Lucille's brother and sister try to upstage her during her ballet performance
on her fourth birthday, but they do not succeed.
ISBN 0-517-80039-X (trade) — ISBN 0-517-80040-3 (lib. bdg.)
[1. Ballet dancing—Fiction. 2. Brothers and sisters—Fiction. 3. Birthdays—Fiction. 4. Pigs—Fiction.]
I. Hafner, Marylin, ill. II. Title.

PZ7.L3274 Sv 2001
[E]—dc21
99-462102

Printed in the United States of America

October 2001

10   9   8   7   6   5   4   3   2   1

First Edition

Lucille's birthday was four days away.

But her grandma's present came early.

She begged to open it right then.

Her older sister, Frances, and brother, Franklin, watched.

"A tutu!" Lucille said. "I'm a dancer!"

Frances shook her head. "I've had ballet *and* tap, Lucille. You don't know any steps."

"I do too know steps," said Lucille.

"Not real ones, the kind you learn in dancing classes," said Frances.

"Who cares?" said Lucille, and twirled around.

"You look stupid," said Franklin.

Lucille didn't listen. She twirled and wore the tutu all day long.

"My, you certainly love that tutu," said Lucille's father that night at dinner.

"I'm going to sleep in it," said Lucille.

"You'll wreck it," said Frances.

"I have an idea," said Lucille's mother. "Let's keep the tutu nice and fresh. Lucille can give a performance on her birthday."

"Yippee!" said Lucille.

So on the first day, Lucille practiced twirling.

On the second day, Lucille
tried leaps and jumps.

On the third day, she
invented a new way to hop.

And on the fourth day, she made up some brand-new
steps and practiced her curtsies.

That night, Lucille dreamed about her performance. She dreamed there was a stage and lights. She twirled. She pranced. She leaped. She hopped. People screamed and clapped. She bowed. She curtsied.

Then she woke up.
It was her birthday!

Lucille could hardly wait to give her performance that night.

First, the family gathered in the living room to give Lucille her presents.

Frances wore her tap shoes. Franklin wore his hockey shirt.

Lucille's father gave her a pair of real ballet slippers. Lucille's mother gave her a sparkly crown.

"Now I'm going to get dressed for my performance," Lucille said.

There was a shriek. Then a roar. "Where's my tutu?" Lucille shouted.

Suddenly, a pink blur flashed by as Franklin rode his bike through the living room. "Look at my hat!" he yelled.

"My tutu!" cried Lucille.

"Who ever heard of a crybaby ballerina?" said Frances. She began to do a tap dance. "This is called the Shim Sham Shimmy," she said.

"Stop dancing!" Lucille yelled at Frances. But Frances kept tapping.

Franklin whooped and crashed into Frances. "My tutu!" cried Lucille.

"Time out!" their mother said. "Give the tutu back *now*, Franklin!"

"It's Lucille's turn," said their father.

"Turn?" said Lucille. "It's my *performance*!"

"Is everyone ready now for Lucille's performance?"
their mother asked.

"I'm going to do three twirls first," said Lucille.

"They're called 'pirouettes,' " said Frances.

Suddenly, the lights went out and beautiful music filled the air.
"Presenting Lucille!" said her father. Lucille twirled, then ran
on her tiptoes and waved her arms very fast. She hummed. "This
is the hummingbird step," she said.

Next, she stood on one leg and
stuck the other high up behind her.

"An arabesque," announced her mother.
Lucille loved the sound of the word. So she
did another one.

"Oooh!" said Franklin.

"So graceful!" said her father.

"Like a butterfly," said her mother.

"That's really good," said Frances.

The music stopped. Everyone cheered and clapped. Even Frances and Franklin.

Lucille bowed and curtsied. Then the lights blinked on and off.

Lucille's mother stood in the doorway holding a birthday cake with four candles and one to grow on.

"Happy birthday to you…," everyone sang.

"Your pirouettes are really good," Frances said.

"I call them 'twirls,'" Lucille answered.

"They were fast," said Franklin.

"Thank you," said Lucille.

Lucille was so tired she put her head
down by her plate and fell asleep before she
ate her cake.

She felt herself being lifted into the air.
She felt the scratchy brush of the tutu and
then the soft fuzz of her pajamas.

She was already dreaming when she thought she heard someone say, "What a day—starring Lucille!"